Money N My Garter

Money N My Garter

Part 1

No Funding

Crystal Nicole

First Media Center hardcover printing edition May 2016 10 9 8 7 6 5 4 3 2 1

ISBN: 1541174291

For information regarding special discounts for bulk purchases, send requests to moneynmygarter@gmail.com.

Printed in the United States of America

This book is dedicated to my daughter, Natiajah, whom I love with all my heart. I told you Mommy had a plan. To all the exotic entertainers who are using the industry to pursue their dreams. To everyone who gave me a place to sleep when I was homeless, and to all those who told me to stop chasing my dreams. Sorry, but I could not do that.

ISBN 13: 9781541174290

"A setback is nothing but a setup for a comeback!"

—*Willie Jolley*

Acknowledgments

First, I want to thank my heavenly father for direction and for the family, friends, and amazing people you put in my life.

Thanks to Kenneth Sessions for the tough love and for challenging me when others would not.

Thanks to Marcella Lewis and Messina Wiseman for editing my book and believing in me.

Thanks to my family. You are fam.

Thanks to my grandparents, who took the time to not only raise me but to take care of my daughter when I went to prison.

Thanks to my niece and nephew for allowing me to spoil and love them.

Thanks to my sisters and brothers for being there when you could.

Thanks to Rick Washington the Hair Spy for being my one-man graphics team.

Thanks to the EDC for my first office space in Prince George's County, Maryland.

Thanks to Lonnell Johnson for providing two office spaces to operate my nonprofit, the Wig Capitol Foundation.

Thanks to my dad for teaching me how to drive.

Thanks to my uncles for loving me like you were my dads. I love you both so much.

Thanks to all who made it possible for me to meet Vice President Biden and his wife, Jill Biden.

Thanks to Dr. Oz for calling me a genius.

Thanks to David Kauffman for investing in and believing in me.

Thanks to everyone who believed in me.

RIP Umar Saunders, Benny Mobley, Micheal McElrath, and Reggie Strayhorn.

1

*R*ing, ring.

"Hello." Quietness filled the phone. "Hello, hello? Who is this?"

"Mom, come get me!" Thirteen-year-old Tiffany cried.

"What's the matter, Tiff? You're scaring me!" her mom replied.

"Dad slapped me in the face because I said to him that he doesn't want me to be with you. I has asked when were we leaving to come visited you and he said we were not going this summer. I was upset and that's what I said to him and he just slapped me. I think he's just scared of me being in the big city."

"Wait - he did what? I'm so tired of your sorry-ass dad! I know that I didn't raise you, he took you from me to be raise by your grandparents in Alabama when you were only six months of age. I can't let this go on any longer. I'm on the next flight to Alabama. Pack your shit!"

Michelle slammed down the phone and didn't give Tiffany a chance to say a word. Tiffany ran to her room to pack the little clothing that she had. She lived with her grandparents and kept only a few items at her dad's place for her weekend visits.

Michelle quickly called her daughter back.

"Don't let anyone know I'm coming."

"Okay," Tiffany replied.

Tiffany rushed down the narrow hallways of the double-wide mobile home to pack her things. She didn't understand why her father was so upset about her going to DC to be with her mom. He would always mention how bad DC was, but Tiffany had never heard or seen of anything bad there. All she knew about it was the tall white building called the Washington Monument, the White House, and about the cherry blossom season. She thought her dad must be a scared country man because he grew up in Alabama and the idea of a big city put fear in him.

Hours passed, and there was still no sign of her mom or her dad. Tiffany finally got tired of waiting, and she lay down on the couch and sobbed impatiently as she waited for her mom to arrive. The next morning, loud bangs on the door woke her up.

"Who is it? Who is it?" Tiffany shouted as she ran to the front door. She wiped the morning cold out of her eyes as she looked through the peephole.

"It's me, your mom. Open up!"

Tiffany opened the door. Michelle stood with her hands on her hips, fire in her eyes, and her 36 double-D breasts wrapped in a T-shirt that read "I Love DC." She looked like Superwoman coming to the rescue with her wet-and-wavy jet-black weave blowing in the wind. Michelle walked past Tiffany into the living room.

"So Jerome still isn't here? It's eight o'clock in the morning. I can't fucking believe your father! Where the hell is his stupid ass?"

"I don't know, Mom. I thought it was him at the door. He didn't come home last night."

"Come on, get your shit. We're leaving!" Michelle looked around the living room at her ex-husband's war pictures that were mounted on the walls.

"So you mean to tell me he left you here alone, no phone call or nothing? Jerome hasn't changed one bit," Michelle mumbled under her breath as she walked outside to the rental car and opened the driver's-side door.

Tiffany loaded her things in the trunk and got in the car with her mother. She couldn't believe her mom had really come for her. She'd been living with her father and his parents all her life, and she'd never really known why she wasn't with her mom. She just knew she wasn't.

"You got everything, Tiff?" Michelle asked as she pressed the starter remote button to turn on the Toyota Camry she'd rented from the Birmingham airport.

"Yes, I have everything," Tiffany said.

As they drove off, Tiffany couldn't help but feel sad because she was leaving her grandparents, who had raised and loved her. She adored her grandparents and didn't want to leave them, but she was ready to leave the country girl behind and to get to know the city life.

"I love you Tiff," Michelle said. "Don't worry. I got you."

An hour later they arrived at the Birmingham airport. Tiffany was very nervous because she had never flown on an airplane before. It took them two and half hours to reach Baltimore–Washington International Airport. In the waiting area, they met a tall, dark-skinned guy who was standing in the distance and waving his hands back and forth as if he were trying to get their attention. Michelle ran up and hugged this six-foot-tall gentleman with snow-white hair that was cut in a fade. He had a smile that lit up the room, with one gold crown on his middle tooth. He was wearing the hell out of his Versace suit, complete with diamond-studded cufflinks. Tiffany looked him up and down. She could smell the money on him.

"How was your flight, baby?" The tall, dark, handsome man asked as he leaned in to kiss Michelle on her right cheek. He stepped back and almost tripped over Tiffany. "Oh, this must be Tiffany," he said as he locked his eyes on her.

Tiffany smiled.

"Tiffany, this is Charles, my coworker" Michelle said with a grin.

"Let's get your bags." Charles walked toward baggage claim. He couldn't help but notice Tiffany's maturing nipples poking through her spaghetti-strap dress and the way the fabric brushed across her petite ass. It made him think about the fetish he had harbored for young girls before he met Michelle. Tiffany could feel his eyes on her. She always had a bad feeling about guys who had gold crowns on their teeth. She thought pimps and drug dealers wore them.

Charles loaded their bags into his BMW 7 Series, and they drove off to one of his three houses in Bowie, Maryland. On the ride to Charles's house, Tiffany and Charles engaged in conversation. He was very talkative and wanted to know where Tiffany's mind was. He always thought he could tell if a girl was a virgin by the tone of her voice. He was attracted to Tiffany, even though he was crazy about Michelle. He couldn't control thoughts of how he used to manipulate young girls like Tiffany to do sexual favors for him. The youngest girl he ever had was twelve years old when he was forty-two. She was his own niece, and now he sends her a monthly allowance to keep her quiet. Michelle thought he was a great uncle, but he knew better.

When they finally parked in Charles's driveway, Tiffany said goodbye and ran to her mother's Beamer, which Charles had bought for Michelle as a Christmas present the year before. Tiffany was ready to explore the city.

2

$\mathcal{L}$iving in the city was more than Tiffany expected. She fell in love with the shopping, the food, and the music, not to mention the fine-ass boys with their "getting-money" attitudes. It didn't take long before the country girl was a city slicker.

Tiffany enrolled in seventh grade in Oxon Hill Middle School, where she quickly became popular. She hung out with Shayla, Danielle, Shemekia, and Trey (he was her only male friend) who all lived in the Shaky Homes neighborhood in Oxon Hill, Maryland. Tiffany loved city life. She loved the skating rinks, go-go parties, and designer clothes. She felt like this was the life she had been missing. Thanks to Tiffany's beauty and country accent, she had no problems with the fellas in.

Trey was one of her closest friend even through he was a guy. She just felt like she could be her country self around him. Secretly Trey had a crush on Tiffany, but was to shy to express his love for her. He would always find himself day dreaming of them being together. Tiffany kinda felt that Trey liked her in more ways then one, but she adored their friendship too much to address it. Trey grew up in a small town in North Carolina, he was the only child. His mom and dad was very prestige people, both his parents had a Master in Business; his father also had a Masters in Communication. Trey was also an excellent dresser, he knew how to make his outfit coordinate with his tennis shoes. He had the best selection of baseball caps, Nikes and Jordan tennis shoes. He would stand in line for hours to get the latest pair.

Tiffany admired the fashion scene of the metropolitan area. Michelle contributed to Tiffany's designer wardrobe. She worked full time at the Library of Congress and part-time as a hair stylist and salon owner. Michelle was a workaholic, which meant she left Tiffany at home alone a lot with her boyfriend, Raymond. With her two careers and her sidemen, she had no time for Tiffany or Raymond. Soon, Michelle and Raymond started arguing constantly. He accused her of cheating with several different men. Maybe it was the weekend getaways or the overnight vacations without him that made him so curious. He blamed Tiffany for his dry season. Since she has moved in he seem to never be able to get any alone time with Michelle and he hated it.

Every afternoon when Tiffany got home from school, she would find Raymond pissy drunk and passed out at the kitchen bar. He would have a bottle of Absolute Gin in one hand and a cigar in the other. One Friday, after school Tiffany noticed Raymond wasn't home yet. (He usually got home from his job at the print shop before Tiffany got out for school) When she walked into the kitchen were Raymond is usually passed out drunk, she stood there and took in a deep breath and exhaling, thinking to herself, I'm glad he is not home. She than decided to freshen up and go downstairs to the basement to watch BET on the sixty-inch television. She picked the cordless phone to call her friend Shayla, who lived next door, to see what she was doing for the weekend. The front door slammed just as Tiffany settled down on the red leather couch that Raymond had bought Michelle for Christmas. Tiffany knew it was Raymond. Who else would be slamming doors and stomping into the kitchen like that?

Raymond was on edge. He'd just gotten off the phone after another argument with Michelle. All he could think about was that Michelle was probably going to leave him again this weekend, and he wasn't having it. Raymond picked up the house phone in the kitchen and started dialing numbers trying to call Michelle back. He didn't realize that Tiffany was on the line, deep in conversation with Shayla.

"Hey Raymond, I'm on the phone," Tiffany said with an attitude. He angrily slammed the phone back on the hook.

"Girl, what's up with that dude?" Shayla asked.

"He's probably drunk, as usual. That seems like the only thing he does around here. I think he's losing it." They both laughed.

"Girl, I hear him coming down the stairs," Tiffany said as she heard the basement door slam behind him.

"I hope Raymond isn't about to start no shit," Tiffany said as she rolled her eyes to the sound of his footsteps.

"When is Rap City coming on?" Shayla asked.

"It should be coming on now," Tiffany replied.

Raymond stood his six-foot-eight-inch frame in front of her, blocking the television. "Get off my damn phone!" he shouted. "Get off my goddamn phone now!"

"Why you tripping?"

"Girl, what you say?" Shayla was still on the line. "He tripping? Do I need to call my brothers on his ass? Cause you know…"

"N'all. I'm straight, Shayla," Tiffany said as Raymond yanked the phone from her ear.

Tiffany went blank for a minute trying to register what had just happened. She looked up at Raymond as he started to walk away. Pissed off, she ran upstairs behind him, cursing. She knew he was drunk, but he had taken it too far this time.

"What the fuck is wrong with you?" she asked. "I just turned sixteen, and I can talk on the phone whenever and how much I damn well please."

"Little girl, you don't pay no damn bills around here, you or your whorish-ass mother," Raymond said. "Where the fuck y'all going tonight? No damn where, and I am going to make sure your mama stay here at home with me. Fucking bitch cheating on me. I know she is."

Tiffany could see in his eyes that he was hurt and upset. She stared at him, wondering why this had to happen while her mother wasn't home.

"Stay off my mother-fucking phone!"

"Raymond, you can't tell me what to do," Tiffany said as she walked into the living room. Raymond and Tiffany argued back and forth as

Raymond took sips from his cup of Absolute. Just as things got heated, Michelle stormed in the front door from a long day's work.

"What the hell is going on here? I can hear you two yelling all the way outside!"

Raymond staggered toward Michelle then stopped to rest his drunken body on the rail behind the couch that separated the living room from the walkway. As Tiffany ran to her mom to tell her what Raymond said, he started yelling.

"I don't give a fuck what you tell your mother, Tiff! I make the fucking rules."

Michelle stood there, stunned. She couldn't believe the way Raymond was talking to Tiffany,

"See, this is why shit is the way it is," Michelle said. "You drunk ass. You stand there half dead talking to my child and me like this. You are worthless piece of a man, and I tried my best to help you."

"Help, my ass!" Raymond shouted. "It's all her fault anyway! Before she came, your ass was home, we spent time together, and hell, if you were cheating, you hid it pretty well. Now you never seem to be home long enough to fuck!" His eyes began to water.

"Fuck you, Raymond. It's not her fault. It's yours. And yes, I tried to help you! I went to counseling with you, drove you to and from AAA meetings just to find out you were not evening going; instead you were walking to the nearest bar and drinking until I picked you back up."

You fucking always drunk! I can't even have a decent conversation with you cause you always fucking drunk. If you want to blame somebody, blame yourself. And far as sex goes, your dick can't get up anyway!"

"Tiffany, get your things. We're leaving!"

"You aren't going anywhere, Michelle!"

"Raymond, I don't have time for this shit. I have to work overtime tomorrow, and I'm tired!" Michelle looked over at Tiffany and then stared at Raymond.

"Tiffany, go get your things now!" Michelle said as she stretched out her left arm pointing down the hallway to Tiffany's room, directing her to go now.

Tiffany wasn't too sure about leaving her mom alone with Raymond.

"Ma, why can't we get our stuff tomorrow?"

"You won't see tomorrow!" Raymond yelled as he grabbed Michelle by her hair and swung her against the wall choking her, "Bitch, I loved you!" he cried.

Tiffany ran toward the phone to call 911, but Raymond tripped her up. She fell flat on her face and passed out. Michelle and Raymond continued to fight. They both fell to the floor. Raymond held Michelle down, choking her even more.

"Bitch, I know you been cheating on me. I followed you. I know that I saw you with that gray-headed man! You must think I'm stupid! You're lucky I haven't fucked the little bitch, as much as you leave her here alone with me while you are out fucking someone else!"

"Raymond!" Michelle shouted as she turned her head away from his salvia that was dripping onto her face. "Stop it!"

"Shut up, bitch!" He yelled as he wrapped his hand more tightly around her neck. "Die you fucking whore!"

Raymond was so occupied with Michelle that he didn't notice that Tiffany had gotten up and was standing over him with a pair of sharp scissors. She swung the scissors toward the back of his head, but when he ducked from the attack, she gashed Michelle in the head. Michelle began to bleed heavily.

"Mom!" Tiffany yelled as she dropped the bloody scissors on the floor. "Mom, are you okay?"

"Tiffany!" Raymond yelled as his reached out to grab her shirt.

Tiffany yelled back at Raymond. "See what you made me do!" She yanked her shirt out of his hand. "I hate you!"

Tiffany ran down the hallway to her bedroom and tried to shut the door behind her, but Raymond stuck his foot in the door to stop her from closing it completely. Michelle thrust her keys at him, but she missed. He turned to her and stared.

"How dare you," he growled.

Tiffany leaned her back against the door with all her weight, but Raymond was still stronger even though he was drunk. "Just leave us alone, Raymond!" Tiffany shouted.

"Raymond, stop!" Michelle muttered. "Just leave her alone!" Raymond pushed the door open, and Tiffany fell to the floor. The door hit the wall so hard that it pierced a hole in the drywall.

"You little bitch. I'm going to fuck you up." Raymond rushed over to Tiffany, picked her up, and threw her on the bed. He pulled at her clothes, tearing her shirt open and forcefully pulling her pants down.

"I'm going to fuck you like you are your mother."

He leaned forward to kiss her but was interrupted when Michelle ran into the room with the bloody pair of scissors that Tiffany had dropped in her hands.

"I will kill you," she said as she raised the scissors in the air.

Ding, dong. Someone was at the door.

Raymond suddenly stopped, and Michelle eased away from him cautiously. Tiffany turned on her knees to crawled towards to the window to looked to see who was at the door. It was two police officers standing in the doorway.

"Mom, don't. It's the police. It's the police!" Tiffany said. "Go, open the door for them. It's the police!"

Silence filled the room, and they all paused and shared puzzled looks. Tiffany hopped off the bed and ran to the front door. Two Prince George's County police officers were waiting outside.

"Please help us!" Tiffany shouted to them. "He's trying to rape me!"

The officers reached for their guns. "Who is trying to rape you? Who's in the house with you?"

"It's me, my mom, and Raymond, my mother's boyfriend." As Tiffany spoke, Michelle and Raymond appeared behind her.

"Ma'am, are you all right?" one officer asked. "I see that you are bleeding." The second officer called for an ambulance.

"What is going on here?" They said simultaneously while they both placed their hands on their guns.

Tiffany explained.

3

After leaving the police station, Michelle went over to Charles's house. Hatred for Raymond welled up in her heart. She didn't care what happened to him anymore. All she knew was that she couldn't raise Tiffany around him. In the same moment good and bad memories of her and Raymond's relationship played in her mind. She remembered the days when they were happy before the alcoholism. After Raymond, brother's death he could not move on and he drunk to ease the pain.

"Mom, where are we going?" Tiffany asked. Her voice was filled with worry.

"Not now, Tiffany! I'm trying to think!"

"I'm sorry. I didn't mean to snap at you. We might have to go to Charles's for the night. It's eleven-thirty, and I'm tired. I'm calling him now to let him know we're on the way."

"Okay, Mom."

"Hello, Charles, it's me," Michelle said frantically.

"What's wrong, Michelle?"

"Raymond and I got into it a huge fight. He also tried to rape Tiffany, and—"

"He did what? I'll kill him! Where is he?"

"He's locked up in the county jail."

"Well, I hope you're pressing charges against that nigga! I told you long ago to leave his ass! What you think, he was going to keep taking yo' shit! I told you he saw us together when we were out to eat at Proud Mary's, and on another night he followed us to Topolino's Restaurant."

"Charles, I don't need to hear this fucking shit," Michelle said. "I have ten stitches in my head, I'm tired, and I just want to lay down! I'm on my way." She hung up the phone, cutting Charles off.

A few months passed, and Michelle realized that she and Tiffany needed their own space. Michelle wanted to enjoy the single life, and jumping into a serious relationship with Charles was not in her plans. They moved into a condo in closer to DC, so Michelle could be closer to her jobs. Tiffany liked the fact that they lived on the border line of DC because she felt like she was right in the middle of the action. She loved hitting the go-go parties to listen to Backyard and them Northeast Groovers and getting in the bed with DC thugs like Cheson, who she met walking to meet up with Shayla. He was a straight street nigga, who stood five nine with cornrows that were long almost reaching he buttocks. His favorite clothes designers were Northface and Hobo Sports gear and wearing a fresh pair of Nike boots. One day when Tiffany was walking her regular route to Shayla's apartment, she heard, "Hey, cutie!" Tiffany looked across the street and saw a group of guys standing at the corner. She ignored the call at first, but then she heard it again, and it seemed closer. She turned around to see who it was or if someone were even talking to her. "He must be calling for me," she thought to herself. "I'm the only girl out here besides this crackhead lady who's crossing the street." The voice called out again, breaking her thoughts.

"Slow down, shorty. What's your name?" There stood Cheson. She immediately was attracted to his cinnamon-brown eyes and his Jay Z lips. Tiffany had a thing for guys with pretty eyes and juicy lips. Cheson stood there admiring her curvy hips that were nicely draped with capri jeans and her tight shirt that exposed her flat belly.

"Where you headed?" Cheson asked with a smirk on his face.

"Excuse me. My name is Tiffany. And you are?"

"Oh, my fault. My name is Cheson, but my friends call me Kane. How old are you?" He asked. "I'm twenty." She added a few years to her real age.

"Oh yeah? Well, I'm twenty-one. Why yo' man got you out here walking?"

"To answer your question I'm walking to meet a female friend of mine because I want to walk," Tiffany said with an attitude as she rubbed her hand through her Janet Jackson in Poet Justice braids.

"I can take you to meet your friend," Cheson said as he glanced at his tinted-out, black-on-black Corvette that sat on twenties.

"Thanks, but no thanks. I don't ride with strangers," Tiffany said as she began to walk off.

Cheson smirked. "I won't be a stranger for long."

"We'll see about that." Tiffany said. She saw Shayla walking toward her.

"What's your number?" Cheson called after her. "Can I call you?"

"I guess so," Tiffany said.

"You can walk over to the car with me if you like."

"Not with all them niggas standing over there. You crazy."

"Cool. Hold on and let me get a pen." Chosen said.

"Girl, he cute." Shayla whispered. "What's his name?"

"Hey, Joey, you got a pen?" Cheson yelled to the crackhead who was opening his car door.

"Yeah, yeah I think I got one. Hey Kane, let me get one, and I'll get you tomorrow."

"Joey, you know better than that. I don't do no loans. You better ask one of them niggas across the street.

"Man, Kane, you so tight!"

"Fuck all that, and hurry up with the pen."

Tiffany stared at him while they waited on the pen.

"Damn, Joey, hurry the fuck up!"

"Hey Tiff, you think you can hook your friend up with my man?"

"I'm not Cupid," she said as he handed her the pen.

By this time, Tiffany wasn't too happy about giving him her phone number. Cheson seemed aggressive, but she like his cockiness. She liked a man who can take control, and it seemed like he had no problem doing that.

4

Tiffany was excited about meeting Cheson she could not wait to tell her friends at school, she finally met a guy. At lunch time she started to tell them all about it. As she was sitting down during lunch at school with her friends in their usual spot telling them all about Cheson, she notice Trey walking towards them, she didn't want him to know what they were talking about.

"What's up Tiff? What's up ya'll?" Trey asked with a big grin on his face.

"We good Trey", they all replied. What's up with you?"

He relied, "nothing waiting on my mom to drop off this pepperoni pizza. You know its Friday and every Friday mom brings me food. That's her work from home day." He said as he playful yanked on Tiffany's school uniform shirt.

"Pizza they all said at once." They then burst out laughing because it was so in tune with each other."

"Your mom is bring you pizza. Damn you spoil! I know you sharing." Tiffany said as she titled her head down peaking her eyes out the top of her eye glasses as she looked at Trey.

"I'll think about," he said cheerful and dashed off.

"Girl Trey is silly, he better be back with that pizza," Shayla said.

"He will," Tiffany said confidently.

During lunch they all decided to walk home with Tiffany after school since she lived the closest to the school, they wanted to hang out.

After having an exciting weekend hanging out with friends and family, Tiffany thought to herself if Cheson does not call me I am just going to walk through that neighborhood again and ask why hasn't he called. As time went on Tiffany started losing hope of hearing from Cheson. Besides it's been a whole week since they have met and he has yet to call.

5

"Tiffany go get the phone." Michelle said as he was unloading the car from a full day at the mall.

"Ok, mom." Tiffany said. The telephone ranged so loud their neighbors can here it.

"Hello," Tiffany stated, "Hello Hello." There was no responds, but right before she hung up the phone she heard a male's voice.

"May, I speak to Tiffany."

"Hello, Hello," she replied.

"Yeah hello may I speak to Tiffany," he repeated.

"Yes, yes this is she. Who is calling?"

"It's Cheson."

"Tiffany who is it on the telephone?" Michelle asked as she stuffed her arms full with shopping bags that covered half of her face.

"It's for me mom."

"Well tell them to call you back and come get these bags!"

"Okay, Mom! Sorry Cheson, could you hold on for one minute. I ll be right back. I just have to put these bags from shopping at the mall today in my room."

"Ok," he said patiently.

They talked for hours, and after that, Tiffany couldn't get enough of hearing from Cheson. After their first date, they were inseparable. Cheson was a baller, and he spoiled Tiffany. He always had a gift for her, whether it was an outfit or a necklace. Since he had been in the drug game for ten years and he had saved up his money, he wasn't hurting for anything. He lived alone in a condo in Southwest DC near the waterfront, and he also rented a small apartment down the street from where he hustled. He owned a Corvette and two SUVs, all suited up with rims, televisions, and banging-ass stereo systems. Dealing with Tiffany slowed him down from running the streets, as she had him wrapped around her finger. Her tight, young, wet pussy had him gone. She would ride his cock until he fell asleep. Tiffany and Cheson were hooked on weed, and he made sure they never ran out. They would get high and have sex anywhere, whether it was in car or behind schools. He couldn't get enough of her.

Months passed, and Cheson and Tiffany were getting more and more serious about each other. He was even thinking about her having his child. Tiffany still hadn't told him her real age yet, and she felt like there was no need to. He knew she was in high school because he would pick her up from school. (Even still he never question her about her age. He knew that some girls lied about their age so he just went with it.) He didn't want any woman of his catching the bus, so he dropped her off and picked her up from school.

One morning, while Tiffany was showering before school, she heard a knock on the door.

"It's open. Come in," she shouted as she stepped out of the shower. It was a little early for Cheson to pick her up.

"Who is it?" she asked as she wrapped her body in a dry towel dripping water all over the floor.

"Who you think it is?" Cheson shouted from the living room.

Tiffany walked out into the hallway to see her man dressed in a white tee and True Religion jeans with her favorite Air Force Is that he had custom made. They were painted in blue and white with the Dallas Cowboys logo engraved on them. His Dallas hat covered his freshly braided cornrows.

"You ain't ready yet. This is why yo' ass is always late and you try to blame me." Cheson said as he plopped down on the edge of her twin size bed.

"Whatever, Cheson." Tiffany laughed. "I just have to dry off and get dressed. Do you want something to drink?" Even though she lived in the city, she still had her southern hospitality.

"N'all, I'm good, but you could bring me a bag to dump this blunt shit in?"

"Okay," she replied.

Tiffany handed him a plastic Walmart bag to dump the blunt shedding in. He started rolling the blunt of weed while Tiffany oiled her petite legs and thighs and her perky tits. Cheson licked the blunt while he watched Tiffany moisturize her camel skin, which made his dick so hard that all his thoughts went to how wet her young pussy would get when she was turned on. Tiffany could feel him watching her.

"Come here, Tiff," Cheson said as he started massaging the area of his pants where his cock lived.

"Don't start. You know I have to go to school."

"Just let me suck on that pussy before you put them panties on."

"No, Cheson. You're going to want to do more than that, and I'm not going to make it to school on time."

"Well hurry up then," he said loudly. His dick went soft. He put on Master P's *Ghetto Dope* and song along with "Thug Girl" as he two-stepped around Tiffany. "Stop playing," she muttered as she searched through her drawer full of colorful panties then out of the blue, her mother stormed into her room.

"Tiffany!" Michelle yelled.

Tiffany turned around, holding an orange and pink thongs. She was stunned to hear her mother's voice.

"Ma!" She frantically searched for something to cover herself with, but nothing was in reach.

"What is this, Tiffany?" Her mother turned the stereo off so she wouldn't have to scream over the music. Tiffany could see the anger in her mother's eyes.

"Cheson, get the hell out! Fucking in my house! You are so fucking disrespectful. You better leave before I call the police!" Michelle pointed to the front door.

Cheson ran past Michelle and out the front door, leaving Tiffany to explain why she was naked.

"Mom, it's not what you think!"

"I don't want to hear that shit. He shouldn't be in the room with you naked, period, or here when I'm not here. Just hurry up and get dressed and get out!"

"Mom, I'm sorry!"

"Just get the hell out!"

Michelle walked to her room, slamming the door behind her. Tiffany slipped into her Coogi designer dress that Cheson had bought her to celebrate their first Valentine's Day together. She put on her black Prada heels and left the apartment. When she got outside, she noticed that Cheson had dropped his hat on the sidewalk. She picked it up and walked toward the parking lot where residents and guests parked, hoping he was there waiting on her.

The sun was beaming bright that morning, and it was about seventy-five degrees. Tiffany really didn't want to be stuck out in the hot sun, but it was only eight o'clock and she had missed the bus and school had already started she had nowhere to go but with Cheson. She put on her Prada frames to hide her eyes, that were red from crying. She didn't want the Cheson to see her crying. When she approached the spot where Cheson usually parked, she was stunned to see he wasn't there. She burst out crying even harding thinking that he had left her. Holding her head in her hands, she heard a horn blow. It was Cheson.

"Tiff, Tiff, where you going?"

She turned her head as he pulled up beside her.

"Get in, baby. What did your mom say?" Tiffany opened the door to the black-on-black Chevy Caprice Classic he had purchased the day before.

"I fucked up, Cheson! She put me out! What am I going to do?" Tiffany cried.

"Don't cry," Cheson said, "It's going to be okay. You can't go to school like this. Say we grab some breakfast and stay in for the day. Besides, school is about to out for the summer, you can always come stay with me."

"Are you sure, Cheson?"

"Yeah, baby, I'm sure," he said with a concerning tone.

Tiffany was glad that Cheson cared enough to allow her to stay with him, but she had never lived with a man before. She was only seventeen years old, and she had always thought that when she did move in with a guy it would be with her husband.

"Trust me, Tiff, it'll be fine," Cheson said as he passed her the blunt of chocolate haze with his other hand caressing her thigh.

When they arrived at his place, Tiffany felt a sense of relief. She sat down on the couch and laid her head back. Her eyes were closed and her legs were wide open. It hurt to know her mom was so upset with her. After all that crying, she just wanted to relax.

Cheson went into the kitchen to pour her a glass of water. He always wanted to show her that he cared. When he got back to the living room, he saw how Tiffany was positioned. He was still turned on from earlier. Cheson sat the glass of water on a glass table that was shaped like the letter S and walked over towards her. He kneeled on the coach and began kissing her neck. He gripped her hair tightly and kissed her plump lips. She wrapped her slim arms around him, pulling him closer. She could see the bulge that indicated his dick was rock hard. She tugged his pants, letting him know that she was aware of its presence. Tiffany yanked his jeans button open, rushing to pull his cock out of the peek of his boxers. Once his cock reached the surface, she shoved his hard cock in her mouth. He looked down to see her bobbing and weaving on his cock, and he leaned his head back and enjoyed every movement she made with her mouth.

"Tiff, Tiff, slow down. You going to make me bust!"

"Shut!" she said.

"Awww...shit," he moaned as his nut rushed down her throat.

He lifted up her dress and pulled her panties to the side, slowly kissing her freshly shaved pussy. She let out a soft moan. She lifted up her dress to watch him in action. She loved the way he ate her pussy, the way he kissed as if he were French kissing her. Her clitoris was throbbing, waiting on his hard dick to make an entrance. He stood tall, and her pussy was soaked by the time he stuck the head of his penis inside.

His pants were unbuckled, so when he stood up from eating her wet pussy they fell down to his ankles. His body jerked as he pressed his way inside of her, and he gave her a few pumps. He pulled his cock out to finger her and then licked the juice from her off his finger. He grabbed her off the couch turning her around to bend her over, inserting his dick from the back. She look back at him to exchange fuck faces. He slowed down to take his shirt off, and while he still was hitting it. He stretched his T-shirt over his head, throwing it to the floor. Cheson's body was slim but muscular, and his six-pack chest and round dark nipples were nice on the eyes. Cheson stood over Tiffany as if he were seven feet tall. She loved how she had to look up to lock eyes when they hugged.

To get more comfortable, he ejected himself from inside of her quickly to step out off his Polo boxers. Before proceeding to thirst Tiffany, he took her by the hand and pulled her to her feet to unlock her body from the doggie-style position. They held hands and kissed as they both breathed heavily. She rubbed her hand down his six-pack as she applied her lips to his left nipple and jerked his wet cock with her hands. She got down on her knees, pulling his boxers down so slowly that she gave his body chills. She sucked his dick as quickly as she could, and when she felt that he was about to come she eased up, licking the tip of his dick because she wanted to tease him.

"Damn! Tiff...don't stop!" he screamed.

She began to suck him slowly again, inch by inch, and all he could feel was pleasure. His knees became weak, and she pushed his body on the coach and sat on top of him. She rode his cock until she climaxed. After she got hers, she jumped off his cock and sucked it again. Cheson was so stiff that he couldn't do anything but admire the movement of her head going up and down. His cock started to pulsate.

"Damn, baby, I'm coming!" he shouted.

She thought to herself, "Damn, I got some bomb-ass head."

He came all over her face. When she realize he was still hard she said, "Fuck my face, baby, fuck my face."

"Damn, bitch," he mumble under his breathe. As sensitive as his dick was, he couldn't turn down Tiffany's vicious head. He rammed his cock to the back of her throat as deep as he could, causing her to gag. He thought to himself, "This is why this bitch can get anything she wants from me." He was hooked. He loved the way she gave herself to him so willingly, and no other girl had ever sucked his dick as well as her. Tiffany did her best to keep him from going elsewhere.

"Damn! I'm coming!" he said for the second time.

6

School was finally ending. On the last day of school all of her friends wanted to meet up at Tiffany's house to spend their last free time together until they met again at school. Shayla, Tiffany and Danielle all were staying in town for the summer while Trey and Shemekia were going to visit their grandparents out of town.

It was a perfect last day of school, the sky was clear, the sun was shinning and the weather was perfect, not to hot and not cold, it had a cool breeze. After meeting up and hanging out with friends, all Tiffany could focus on is her moving in with Cheson. She wonder to herself was she too young to move out and live with a man, will it work and could she really deal with the pressures of dating a street thug.

Tiffany knew there was something special about Cheson, but she never expected to bear his only child. They were together for one years before she got pregnant with their baby girl, Lazia. Tiffany was excited about carrying his first child. She hoped that having his baby would mean they would get married and he would get off the streets and into the corporate world.

Cheson had been slinging heroin, crack cocaine, and whatever other drugs out there that would make a fast buck. The game was how he ate, slept, and shit. All of sudden he started doing a drug call Phencyclidine better known as PCP. Things got hacked between the two after he started to get high off of PCP, which caused problems between him and Tiffany. He also beginning drinking alcohol a lot after his cousin, Mike, got killed by Cheson's best friend from tripping off of PCP. Tiffany didn't like it when he got drunk because he would start fights with her or anybody else who got in his way. Tiffany didn't do any major drugs. She tried PCP a few times with Cheson and her friend Shayla, but it made her sick to the point of vomiting, so she stopping using it. One time she tripped so hard that she thought she was walking down stairs where there was no stairs. After that, she knew she couldn't make smoking PCP a habit. She did drink but not as much as Cheson. Her favorites were Remy Martin and Moet every now and then, but it was weed that she loved the most.

The PCP made Cheson forgetful, and he would beat Tiffany until she turned black and blue. He wouldn't remember a thing the next day. She was getting tired of getting her ass whooped. After the baby was born, she hoped that he would change for the better, but he didn't. Cheson was paranoid that she would leave him after the baby was born once she got her figure back. She wanted to leave him, but it wasn't until he started beating her in front of their eight-month-old baby girl that Tiffany found the courage to fight back. Her thoughts of leaving him grew stronger.

One day, Tiffany was getting herself and Lazia ready to go out Hains Point Park with her friend Jessica. Cheson stormed into the bedroom after being out on the block all night. He smelled like straight liquor and weed. He tossed all the money he had made the night before on the bed. "Count this!" he ordered.

"I don't want to count your money, Cheson! Me and the baby are getting ready to go out. Jessica is on her way to pick us up," Tiffany said as she finished snapping the baby's diaper.

"Where you taking Lazia?" he asked.

"Jessica is taking me and Lazia to Hains Point."

"I can take y'all. Just let me take a quick shower," he said as he sat down on the edge of their king-size bed and kicking off his Timberland boots.

"That's okay, Cheson. Why don't you stay here and chill?"

"I don't need to chill," he said, stumbling to get back to his feet.

"Cheson, please, just lay down."

"Hold up. You don't tell me what the fuck to do. I tell you what the fuck to do. I run shit around here!"

"Damn, you're scaring the baby!"

"You not taking my baby nowhere, especially with that bitch Jessica. I know she be hooking you up with niggas and shit. I don't trust that hoe!"

"Why you got to trip? We're just going to park. Damn! Besides, it's nice out, and it's the fourth of July. When we get back, we can go see the fireworks."

"I'm not stupid, Tiff. You ain't about to drop my baby off with that bitch so you can go fucking around!"

"It ain't even like that, Cheson. Why are you so fucking paranoid? You need to stop smoking that shit! I told you I'm not cheating!"

"You ain't going!" he said as he took off his shirt.

"Why not, Cheson? It would be nice to take her to the park. We both need some fresh air. Plus we have been cooped up in this house all day," Tiffany said as she waved her hand in front of her nose to wave away the stench coming from Cheson.

She grabbed her purse and the baby bag. As she reached for Lazia, who was sitting in her walker, Cheson pulled Tiffany by the hair and threw her on the bed.

"Bitch, I told you, you ain't taking my baby nowhere!"

He stared at her for a second, and before she knew what was what, he punched her in the mouth, splitting her bottom lip. She burst out crying, not from the pain but more so understanding how the man she loved and the father of her child could treat her so badly. She felt like she was in a Lifetime movie.

"Why you got to hit me in front of her? I hate you," she screamed.

He struck her again. For the first time she said to herself I am leaving him for good. She proceed to fighting back. She kicked him as hard as she could in the stomach. He wrapped his arm around his waist. Tiffany leaped off the bed. She ran toward Lazia, who was screaming at the top of her lungs. Cheson reached for Tiffany again, pulling her shirt and making her fall.

"Bitch, I'll kill you if you leave here with my daughter!" he screamed as he kicked her. His cousin, who was sleeping in the next room, ran in to Chevon's room to find out what was going on.

"Man, let her go! Your daughter's watching this shit! You don't hear her crying?" He cousin stated.

Cheson stopped beating her. Tiffany was in so much pain that she could barely get off the floor. She took Lazia out of the walker as quickly as she could and limped out of the front door with her purse and baby bag in hand. She was grateful when the city bus pulled to the bus stop, and she got on the bus as quickly as she could.

"Tiff, please get off the bus. I'm sorry! Don't leave me like this!" he begged.

He must have known it was really over and she wasn't going to take his shit any longer.

"Look at me, Cheson! I'm all bloody and shit," she said as she pointed to her bruised face.

"Just go! Leave us the fuck alone! It's over!"

"Miss, do you want me to call the police?" the bus driver asked.

"N'all, man, you don't have to call the police. I'm getting off." Cheson headed toward the door.

"It ain't over, Tiff," he said with a mug look on his face.

Cheson threw a roll of one-hundred-dollar bills wrapped in a rubber band into her lap. "Take that for my baby. You'll be back!"

Tiffany rode the bus to Jessica's apartment. She could hardy knock on the door. Jessica was already on her way out to pick them up after dropping off Cheson's friend Moe at Southview apartments.

"Girl, what happened? How long have you been at the door? I didn't hear you knocking." Jessica picked up Tiffany and Lazia off the floor. What's wrong why you and the baby are sitting the floor, why is you look like you just got done fighting, she said as she walked with them into her living room. Jessica sat Lazia in the baby swing that she'd kept in her apartment for when she babysat her. Jessica was a good godmother; she had baby things everywhere.

"I can't take this shit anymore. I am tired of Cheson beating on me. How did it get to this? We used to be so happy!" Tiffany cried.

"Girl, that nigga crazy. It ain't you. It's them damn drugs. Plus, he all depressed about his cousin getting killed. Ever since that happened, he just has been spaced out. Moe even mention it to me about how he be smoking dippers back to back."

"You know, that crazy-ass nigga probably on his way over. I know you told him I was picking y'all up. Moe is on his way to bring me some money, and I just dropped his ass off. Me and his crazy ass got into it last night because he always wants to use my car and not put gas in it. Girl, we went out the other day, and he cursed me out in front of everybody at the movies because he thought I was looking at another nigga. I told him that it's over. He's just giving me my keys back and half the rent. You know, Momma wants her money."

"What? You didn't tell me that!" Tiffany replied, trying to focus on Jessica's issues for the moment instead of hers.

"Cheson ain't coming up here anyway. He got to go out B-more in an hour to pick some shit up. You know he's not going to let me stop his money. Let me use the phone. I'm calling my mom."

"Girl, you know Ms. Michelle gonna be pissed off. You can stay here if you want. You know my mom ain't gonna trip. Besides, she never here no way."

"Girl, no, this is too close for comfort. I need to get out of the city for a while and go back home with my mom. I'm tired of this crazy life. I can't raise Lazia around this shit."

"I know, girl, she don't need to be around yo' baby daddy's dip-out ass," Jessica said as she handed Tiffany the cordless phone.

"Mom, can I come back home?"

"Sure, Tiff. I have been waiting for this day."

"Cheson beat me up pretty bad."

"He what? Has he been hitting you all this time?"

"No, Ma, but he has for the last three months."

"Where are you? I'm on my way to come get you."

"I'm at Jessica's."

"Why didn't you catch a cab here? You only went up the street from him, and he could be there any minute."

"He's not coming."

"Be ready. I'm on the way!" Michelle quickly hung up the phone.

Once Tiffany got in the car with her mom, she knew she was going to get lectured. She felt like she might need a lecture. It had been a while since she'd talked to her mom, let alone gotten advice from her.

"Tiffany you can't go back to that. You can't raise my grandchild in no abusive home. I'm not having that!"

"You're right, Mom. That's why I want to stay with you until I can get out on my own."

"Tiffany that's not a problem. Cheson is a problem. He could have killed you. I knew that nigga wasn't about shit. Maybe you need to move back to Alabama until everything dies down."

"I think that would be good," Tiffany said as she looked out the window and watched the building go by. "I need to get my mind right."

The next morning, Michelle booked Tiffany on a flight to Alabama.

7

efore Tiffany left for Alabama, she wanted to spend time with Jessica, who had always been a good friend to her. Jessica and Shayla had taken Tiffany under their wings when she had first arrived at Oxon Hill Middle School.

So far, there had been no sign of Cheson. Tiffany thought she was in the clear. He didn't call her, stalk her, or try to see Lazia. She thought that he had finally let her go until the day she and Jessica decided to walk back to Jessica's apartment after picking up Chinese take out. Jessica started to run when she spotted Cheson and Moe walking toward them.

"Why you running?" Tiffany asked as she tried to catch up.

"You didn't see them?" Tiffany turned to see Cheson and Moe on their tails.

"Hurry up, girl, so I can lock the door!"

"Let us in!" Moe screamed as he banged on the door.

"No, go away!" Jessica shouted back.

Suddenly, the banging stopped. They thought the coast was clear. Tiffany and Jessica pushed a dresser in front of the front door in hopes of blocking it, just in case they didn't give up that easily. Suddenly there was the sound of the balcony door opening.

Oh shit, Jessica said as she looked back to see Moe pulling back the blinds that covered the balcony door. Then, they ran to Jessica's bedroom, she locked the door behind them and they hid in her walk-in closet, terrified. Once Moe got inside, he pushed the dresser away from the door that was barricaded to let Cheson in. Cheson yelled out Tiffany's name as if he were Tarzan in the jungle. They ran toward Jessica's room and kicked down the door, leaving it hanging on its hinges. Tiffany and Jessica were horrified. Moe remembered how big the closet was because he'd hidden in there many of times, to hide from Jessica's mother. When he opened the closet door, he found Jessica and Tiffany holding one another and rocking back and forth fearfully. Cheson grabbed Tiffany by the hair, dragged her out of the closet and squeezed her neck tightly, choking her. Tiffany struggled to get free, but he wouldn't let go. His grip just got tighter and tighter.

"Where's my baby?" Cheson yelled, squeezing her neck. "Bitch, have you been cheating on me? Tell the truth."

"No, baby!" Tiffany squealed. "I love you!" she said as she felt herself passing out. Cheson quickly loosened his grip and let go of her throat as her body went limp on the bed. He tapped on Moe's shoulder, indicating he was ready to go. Moe, who was also choking Jessica, let go. "Stupid bitch!" he said. "All you had to do was open the fucking door."

Cheson and Moe fled the scene, hoping no one had seen or heard them. Jessica crawled from the closest and saw Tiffany passed out on the bed.

"Tiff, Tiff, wake up! Please wake up!" Jessica said. Tiffany coughed and tried to catch her breath. "I thought I was going to die," Tiffany said as she wept. The girls held each other and cried.

The next day, Tiffany and Jessica decided to go to the mall early. They didn't want to face Jessica's mom and have to tell her what happened. When they returned to Jessica's apartment that afternoon, they were shocked to find fire trucks, police vehicles, and ambulances everywhere. Jessica's apartment has been set on fire. Jessica ran to the front of her apartment entrance and burst into tears. There were rose petals leading out of her apartment. Tiffany put her arms around Jessica to console her. Jessica screamed, "my mom is going to kill me!"

8

After arriving in Alabama, Tiffany became depressed about what had happened to Jessica. She was worried that Moe would try something else crazy to harm her. He wasn't wrapped too tightly. Moe was a short, stocky guy who wore his hair cut low. He had a dark brown complexion. Tiffany didn't think he was cute at all, but she was glad he and Jessica had hooked up because Cheson and her enjoyed double dating with them. Jessica really didn't have good taste in boys. She either liked the boys with a criminal history and long hair who wore their pants down to their knees and exposed their boxers or she liked the boys who were clean cut but had a bad-boy mentality.

Tiffany really cared for Cheson and didn't want to leave him, but she had done what she thought was best for Lazia and herself. Everything was going fine with her grandparents. They were proud of Tiffany. Even though she'd had a baby at seventeen, she was doing very well in school and was at the top of her class.

Tiffany stayed in Alabama for a year and attended Greene County High School. She got her first job, working as a nail technician, at the popular Germaine's Hair Salon. Her grandparents were so strict that working at the hair salon and going to school were the only times she was able to go into town. She couldn't wait to get back to DC.

To create space, she snuck out in the middle of the night while Lazia was sound asleep to hang out with friends and mingle with boys. She could never fight her love for smoking weed. She did her best to keep her mind off Cheson. She missed him, but mostly she missed the sex. She often found herself tucked away in a bathroom masturbating to the memories of their great sex. Even though she had a new boyfriend in Alabama, he couldn't compare to what she had with Cheson.

9

uring her year back in Alabama, Tiffany met a guy named Lamont. He was one of the few guys she dated while she was back in her hometown. She had harbored a crush on him since she was in elementary school. She always tried to pass him in the hallways on their way to and from class. Back then, she was too shy to express how she felt. She was just an eleven-year-old girl. Lamont was handsome. Even as a little boy, he stood out with his high-yellow skin tone, beautiful smile, and a mole below his left cheek. He was kind of short and wore a high-top fade.

Their relationship lasted for two years before things went sour. Lamont started mentally and physically abusing Tiffany. He was a full-time student at the University of Alabama, so she blamed it on the fact that his studies was stressing him out. She constantly forgave him until she realized the abuse had become a pattern. She confronted Lamont about it and told him that he either had to stop the abuse or she was leaving him. She didn't want the same thing to happen with their relationship as had with Cheson, however, so she unexpectedly stopped over at Lamont's mom's house, where he stayed on the weekends. Tiffany called him from her cell phone.

"I'm out back. Come open the door," she said, her voice sad and depressed.

He opened the door to find Tiffany wearing a black baseball cap, a loosely fitted Baby Phat sweat suit, black slippers, and her favorite Louis Vuitton backpack.

"What you doing out here in the rain with them damn slippers on?" Lamont asked. "Here she goes with the same ole' bullshit," he thought to himself.

"Are you okay?" he asked. Tiffany's eyes began to tear up. "What's the matter, Tiff?"

"We need to talk," Tiffany said as she walked into the kitchen.

"Let's go in my bedroom," Lamont said, resting his hand in the arch of her back and directing her toward his bedroom.

"What are you doing?" she asked as she stepped over a pile of pictures on the floor.

"I'm cleaning out my closest," he replied.

Tiffany sat on the edge of his bed and prepared her thoughts. Then she noticed a picture of a naked woman peaking out of a pile he had scattered on the floor. He bent down to snatch the nude picture up before she could grab it. She reached over Lamont's shoulder to grab the picture out of his hand. He turned around, hitting her in her mouth with his Movado watch. Her lip started to swell. Tiffany grabbed her backpack and stormed out the back door. Fired up and hurt mentally and physically, she was wanted revenge. Besides, how's she was going to explain her bruised lip to her grandparents, her family, and her daughter? Before she went home, Tiffany stopped by her friend Olivia's house to calm down.

Olivia lived right down the street from Lamont. Tiffany needed a shoulder to cry on. She was tired of Lamont cheating and abusing her. She parked her uncle's yellow 1995 Cadillac Eldorado, which he allowed her to drive to visit Lamont, behind Olivia's apartment in case Lamont drove by. She didn't want him to know where she was.

After she parked the car, she sat and cried for what felt like hours. In actuality, it was only a few minutes before she mustered the strength to walk to Olivia's door. She knocked, her head hanging down to hide the tears that were running down her face.

"Who is it?" Olivia asked politely.

"It's Tiffany," she replied.

Olivia opened the door. "Girl, what's up? Damn, what the fuck happened to your lip?"

"Lamont hit me..."

Before she could even get it all out, Olivia said, "Let's fuck this nigga up. I am tired of him treating you like shit. Who the fuck does he think he is? Let's go fuck up his car tonight." They walked toward her bedroom.

"I do want to get back at him," Tiffany said. "You're right. Let's go fuck his car up."

"Girl, Lamont will kill you for banging up his Volkswagen."

"Well, that will teach him not to put his damn hands on me like that again."

"Okay, we have to plan this. Let's go around four a.m., when we know the town is pretty much asleep. You don't want anybody seeing us pulling up at his house. We're just going to pull into his next-door neighbor's house. They are up in age and probably sound asleep."

"Great," Tiffany said, nervous as all outdoors. She had never done anything like this before. She had heard her uncles and her dad talk about women slicing tires and breaking windows, but she never thought she would end up doing it.

At around four a.m., Olivia drove her 1996 Honda Accord to Lamont's to make it easier for Tiffany to jump out and do her thing. They pulled up in next-door neighbor's yard and saw Lamont's car parked behind the shed, which was one of Tiffany and Lamont's favor sex spots. Tiffany ran over to the car with a crowbar in one hand and a knife in the other. She swung, bashing the front windshield and then the driver- and passenger-side windows. The sound of the broken glass reminded her of the cracks in her heart. Tiffany slashed all four tires, and after the damage was done she felt vindicated.

"Hurry up!" Olivia shouted out of her car window.

Tiffany ran back to the car with her heart in her lap, breathing as if she had just run a marathon. Once she caught her breath, she thanked

Olivia for watching her back. Tiffany decided to take the long way home, not ready to face the consequences of keeping her uncle's car out all night. She lit up the blunt of high-dro weed that she had hidden from Olivia. She knew after fucking up Lamont's car that she would need to take a blunt to the head.

The next morning, Tiffany was awakened by the house phone ringing off the hook. She knew it was Lamont, so she cut the ringer off. She wasn't ready to deal with him yet. As she was getting ready to go to work, her grandfather approached her about what had taken place the night before.

"Tiffany, what happen to Lamont's car? I tried to use the phone, and Lamont was on the line screaming your name. Now, Tiff, you gonna have to go back to Maryland with this shit. I'm not taking this bullshit!" her grandfather yelled.

Tiffany quit her job at Germaine's, and she left for Maryland the following week.

10

ow that she was back in Maryland, Tiffany prayed that the abuse was out of her life. Once she got to her mom's place, she became determined to stand on her own two feet. She was tired of depending on guys to love and take care of her. She felt like she could do it herself. Within her first week of being back home, she was hired as a salesperson at Shoe City in Iverson Mall. She wasn't too excited about selling shoes, but she figured this job was better then nothing. She dreamed about starting her own business. She had thought about going into business for herself since she was a kid. At a young age, she had helped her grandparents do paper work for the family farming business. She admired her grandfather for being his own boss. He always walked around with large checks, and everywhere he went people would call him boss. She loved that. Her grandfather was a boss, and she wanted to be one too.

Tiffany had always wanted to own a beauty-supply store. She was fascinated with how people could go to a place other than a hair salon to enhance their looks. But most beauty-supply stores were owned by Koreans. Tiffany repeatedly asked her mom to start the business for her so she could run it. She even asked her grandparents, but she was turned down every time. "I don't know nothing about running a beauty supply store," her mom would say. "I own a hair salon, and that's it."

Even though she couldn't get her family to back her, Tiffany knew in her heart she would eventually find a way. She never gave up on the idea of being her own boss.

While working at the shoe store, a guy stopped in and handed out fliers that read,

"4 PLAYERS STRIP CLUB HIRING DANCERS NO EXPERIENCE NECESSARY."

"This could be the way to get the funding I need to open my first retail store," Tiffany thought. She stuck a flier in her back pocket.

"Girl, are you going to do it?" said her ex-friend Danielle, who also worked at the store. "You know Tasha is dancing now. She was dancing when we were in middle school."

"Shut up! No she wasn't," Tiffany said with an attitude.

"She was. Remember when she was staying with me after her mother put her out?"

"Yeah," Tiffany said, rolling her eyes.

"Well, Tasha used to always carry this big suitcase out with her. Sometimes she would leave my house and call me late at night to open the door for her so she wouldn't wake my mom. She would always make sure she was gone before my mother came home. So one night after she fell asleep, I went through that bag and found all this lingerie stuff, sexy boots, and even handcuffs. She also had a fake ID."

"For real?" Tiffany said, so shocked she could not believe it.

Tiffany wasn't really trying to communicate with Danielle. They had had a falling out over some nude pictures that Tiffany had given to Cheson. The photos had somehow gotten into Danielle's hands, and she had shown them to every guy at the school. Tiffany could not understand how a friend could spread rumors about her and show off her private pictures. Tiffany stopped speaking to her. Now that they were both working at the shoe store, she had to talk to Danielle from time to time.

Danielle felt bad about what she had done to Tiffany. She begged Tiffany to forgive her and said she wanted to be friends again. Danielle had become close to a friend of Tiffany's, and the friend told Tiffany that Danielle was always kind to her. After some time had passed, Tiffany reconsider and they became friends again.

11

Tiffany never answered Danielle's question about dancing at the strip club. She often pulled the flier out and looked it, imagining what it would be like to work there. Even though she was beautiful she felt insecure because of the stretch marks on her stomach. Her stomach was like Jell-O and was covered with stretch marks she hated it. Tiffany thought she looked more like a woman in her eighties than the eighteen-year-old that she was. "How can I dance with a belly like this?" she thought to herself. Chosen use to always say to her that her belly after the baby was like his pillow that it was so soft and beautiful. One day, Tasha came into the store to shop. Tiffany was impressed with her designer outfit, stunning shoes, and $2,500 Gucci handbag.

"Hey, Tiffany, is that you? I thought you moved back to Alabama."

"I did. I just got back like two weeks ago."

"Damn, and you got a job already. I know that's right. How is Lazia? I know she got big. You still messing with Cheson?"

"Yeah, she got big, and hell no, I ain't messing with that crazy-ass nigga. He doesn't even know I am back, so please don't tell him," Tiffany whispered as if Cheson could hear her.

"Girl, I haven't seen that nigga since middle school, since that day he dropped you off and you came to school late and was bragging on how he was eating your pussy all night."

"Yeah, I remember that. The boy sure could eat." Tiffany said with a grin. They both burst out laughing.

"Well, girl, I hear you dancing."

"Yeah, I been dancing since middle school. Danielle told you, didn't she?"

"How? You was only sixteen years old."

"I know, Tiff. Fake IDs work. I can get you one." Tiffany looked at Tasha, and they both started to giggle.

"Have you ever heard of 4 Players? It's a strip club on Beech Road that just opened."

"N'all, I never heard of it. Why are you dancing now?"

"No, not me. I can't. My body too messed up after having Lazia."

"Girl, that don't mean shit. You have a pretty face and a beautiful smile, that will get you by. You would be surprised to see how them girls' bellies look at the clubs."

"How so? I thought guys go to the club to see fine-ass girls with sexy bodies."

"I'm telling you, them girls ain't got shit on you."

"If you say so."

"Well, I'm getting out of here. I don't see anything I want. I really came to see you. Danielle told me you were back in town and you two work together. I wanted to go see my girl. Here is my number. Call me sometime. I'll treat you to lunch, or we can go somewhere and get our nails done or something."

"Okay." Tiffany smiled. She was happy to see Tasha.

Tasha's big, round ass looked like a donkey's butt as she walked away. Tasha was a sexy, chocolate-brown brick house. She had high cheekbones from the little bit of Indian in her family, and she had a petite body and small, set-up breasts. Her butt look bigger than it had in middle school. She was bad to the bone.

12

"Hey, Tasha, how are you? Did you want to come over to see the baby?" Tiffany asked.

"Yeah," Tasha replied. "Thanks for calling. By the way, I was just thinking about you. I'm just passing where your mom use to stay. Do y'all still stay over there behind the IHOP on Saint Barnabas Road?"

"Yeah, we do."

"Okay, I'll stop by before I go to work. Do you think your mom would mind me getting dressed for work over there?"

"I don't think so."

"Okay, great. I'll see you soon."

Hours passed, and finally the door belled rang. Tiffany rushed over after laying Lazia on the coach. She had just put her to sleep.

"Hey, Tasha. I didn't think you were coming."

"Girl, I told you I would."

"Hey Ms. Michelle. How you doing?"

"I'm fine," Michelle said as she looked at Tasha's nice figure through the top of her eyeglasses.

"How you been?" Michelle asked.

"I'm good. Just got my car out of the shop."

"You got a car? Girl, where you working at? You need to help Tiffany get a job."

"Mom, I told you Tasha dances."

"So what. You should try it."

"Mom!"

"I'm just saying if it would help you more than that Shoe City job, you should give it a try. You need a car and more."

"Really, Mom, you would let me do that?"

"You grown. You have a baby to take care of. You need to get your own place."

"Look at my stomach, Tiffany said as she pulled her Shoe City work shirt up to reveal her belly covered with stretch marks.

"Girl, there is nothing wrong with your stomach," Tasha said. "I am telling you there are girls I work with in the club who bellies are worse than that."

"Worse than this?" Tiffany questioned.

"Yes, and they make money."

"I am telling you, them guys ain't tripping off that."

"Okay, then I'm going to try it."

After Tasha left, Tiffany put Lazia in the room with her mom so that she could practice dancing in front of the mirror in her bedroom.

13

After work on Thursday, Tiffany was getting herself ready. She didn't really know what to expect. She had decided that afternoon that she would go to tryouts. She called her mom from the Shoe City store phone.

"Hey, Mom, I'm going to tryouts after work."

"Tryouts for what?"

"The club."

"How are you getting there?"

"Well, I was going to ask Danielle if she were going to try out too so I could ride with her. She is the one who told me about Tasha and said I should dance too."

"Okay, Tiff. I'll see you when you get home."

"Are you serious, Mom? You want me to do this?"

"Hon, you got to do what you got to do. It's legal."

"Okay. Danielle just walked past me. I've got to go." I called out to Danielle. "You on lunch yet?"

"No," she said.

"Do you want to go to tryouts today at that 4 Playa Club? You know, the flier we got?"

"That's funny. I was going to ask you about it too."

"I'm thinking about," I said.

"Well, let's see if we can take our lunch break at the same time and go to the lingerie store and buy outfits."

"All right, cool. Lunch then."

Three hours passed, and it was time for them to go to lunch. Tiffany had only worked at Shoe City for one month, and this was the first time she and Danielle had been to lunch together. Tiffany was finally letting her guard down and allowing their friendship to rebuild.

"We have to hurry up and get the outfits cause I'm hungry," I said. "I want to eat."

"Me too," Danielle replied.

When they reach the lingerie store that was around the corner, Tiffany was happy to see all of the dance clothes and the variety of lingerie. Now she could play up her femininity to the fullest. She had always thought that because she was a black girl she had to be a little masculine to show strength. Now, she could be as feminine as she wanted to be and get paid doing it.

"I want those black garter belts. They'll go with anything," Tiffany told the cashier. "Give me the white and the red garter belts too. I prefer to switch things up.

"Also, do you sell fishnet stockings?"

"Yes," the cashier replied. "Over there on this wall."

Tiffany walked over to the wall and selected red, white, neon-green, and neon-pink stockings.

"Okay, I got what I wanted. What are you getting, Danielle?"

"I'm getting this thong-and-bra set with the gold on it. I think gold would look nice next to my dark skin."

Once lunch was over, it was countdown time. They both were anxious to get off work and go home to get ready for the auditions. Danielle walked over to Tiffany as she was restocking the T-shirt island.

"Hey, I'll help you finish," Danielle said. "I already straightened up the shoes in the back. Does your mom know you going to dance?"

"I told her about it. She's the one that told me to try out after Tasha came over talking about all the money and fun she was having."

"Well, I hope we make some money. What time should I pick you up? They said tryouts start at six p.m."

"Come get me about five forty-five. I stay right around the corner from the place."

"You sure do. Okay, I'll be there."

"Cool."

Counting down the minutes until she got off work, Tiffany found herself thinking about what the club scene would be like.

Made in the USA
Middletown, DE
05 September 2023

37932669R00033